**Clint Faraday**
book twenty nine
*Grave Responsibility*

Salvatore Santos, a good friend on the comarca at Cusapín, calls Clint to say he's being held in jail in Chiriqui Grande. He is charged with his brother's murder!

That doesn't make any sense, but some gringo said he'd heard him confess. In Panamá, you're guilty until proven innocent. He didn't doubt he could do that, but who would take care of his family while he was in jail?

# Contents

# About the author

CD Moulton has traveled extensively over much of the world both in the music business, where he was a rock guitarist, songwriter and arranger and in an import/export business. He has been everything from a bar owner to auto salvage (junkyard) manager, longshoreman to high steel worker, orchid grower to landscaper, tropical fish farmer to commercial fisherman. He started writing books in 1983 and has published more than 350 books as of January 1, 2023. His most popular books to date are about research with orchids, though much of his science fiction and fantasy work has proven popular. He wrote the CD Grimes, PI series, and the Det. Nick Storie series, Clint Faraday series, and many other works.

He now resides in Gualaca, Chiriqui, Panamá, where he writes  books, plays music with friends, does research with orchids and medicinal plants. He has lately become involved in fighting for the rights of the indigenous people, who are among his closest friends, and in fighting the extreme corruption in the courts and police in Panamá.

He offers the free e-book, *Fading Paradise*, that explains what he has been through because of the corruption.

CD is the discoverer of the Chadam Protocol for curing cancer.

Facebook page Ambrosia peruviana for cancer.

## Grave Responsibility

### <u>Questionable Statement</u>

Clint Faraday, retired PI from Florida, now living in Panamá, looked out over the calm Caribbean from Cusapín and sighed contentedly. This was paradise. Much of Panama was paradise, but this was special. His wife and two month old baby, Clintonito, called Nito, were giggling and cooing in the kitchen.

It was getting expensive. He was glad he had made so much (by accident) with his cases, here. It wouldn't hurt him, but it definitely wouldn't be good for most others, particularly those living on pensions.

He stepped off his porch and went down to the dock and into his boat to get the tackle and catch, cleaned the boat, cleaned the fish, and gave it to Tyna to cook for lunch, cleaned the tackle, then swam in the crystal water for a few minutes before climbing onto the beach and rinsing off under the homemade shower by the porch. Judi Lum, his attractive Oriental neighbor in Bocas del Toro and major help in the detective work, called to tell him she was going to Las Tablas with Dave (their nutty botanist/ musician/writer friend) and Selma, Dave's regular ladyfriend. She lived there, Dave lived several places in Panama. Ben and Earl, neighbors, would take care of the orchids for her while she was gone. He said to have a safe trip, and went in to catch up on his e-mail. Four legitimate ones along with fourteen spam. Normal.

It was just seven fifteen AM, so he would putter and fix things around the place.

His phone rang. He answered to hear, "Clint? Salvatore Santos. I don't know who else to call, but I'm in jail in Chiriqui Grande."

"In jail? What for?"

"They claim I murdered my brother."

"Your brother? Jesus? He's dead?"

"Yes. He is dead. He was drowned, so it was probably that someone killed him, because he knew the water and the dangers as well as any-one. I only need to have someone take care of my family until this is fixed. I haven't killed anyone, never to think of killing my own brother. I wasn't even out in my boat when he drowned, so I couldn't have done it."

You are guilty until proven innocent in Panama, but Clint didn't see how they could arrest Sal. He was a very easygoing, peaceful type.

"Why did they arrest you? They must have a reason. Did you and Jesus argue or anything?"

"No, Clint. Everything was as it always was. Jesus was worried about something, but I didn't think it was serious, but that must be wrong. Some gringo said I had confessed! I don't even know him! I never talked to him, except once at the China, when he asked about something when they found Jesus dead. He asked about ... something. I said whatever was the answer, just a curious person asking, I thought.

"Can you help me with the family for a couple of days? They arrested me right here in Chiriqui Grande and Yajaira and Nica can't get back to Cusapín without me."

"Of course. I'll come to Chiriqui Grande right away, and can bring them back to Cusapín, then I'll come back there and find out what the hell is going on. That seems a questionable reason to arrest anyone, to me. Some gringo who ... does the gringo speak Spanish?"

"Maybe a little. I speak some English."

"He's made what I can only call a questionable statement. I'll try to get to the bottom of it."

"Thank you, Clint. I really appreciate your help. I don't know anyone else who can help."

"De nada! I'll pick up Yajaira and Nica in about forty five minutes. Can you tell them to be at the dock?"

"Jorge is a friend. In the police. He'll tell them to go there to wait for you."

Clint hung up and stood to think. This was a bit strange, even for the system. What reason would some gringo have to cause an Indio to be charged with murder? He changed, called Ben, a neighbor, to say Judi said he'd take care of his and Judi's plants if he didn't get to Bocas Town soon, then headed for Chiriqui Grande. He picked up Sal's wife and son, took them back to Cusapín, and was back in Chiriqui Grande just as the sun was setting. He checked into the pensión, had a good meal, then went to see Sal, who was sitting in the station office with Jorge Divas and Raul Menendez, drinking coffee. They didn't discuss Sal's case much, saying the declarations and legal papers would be ready in the morning when Clint could read them to see what the Sam hell was happening. It was all too possible there was just a misunderstanding. The gringo, Earl Smelters, didn't speak very much Spanish, and Sal was far from fluent in English.

"What did he claim?" Clint asked.

"He said that he asked Sal about his brother and that Sal said he was responsible for Jesus being dead, or something.

"We don't believe Sal killed anyone. We can

work it out in the morning. Maybe Sal just told them he told Jesus not to go out today, so he was responsible because he didn't stop him, but Sal says there was no reason to tell Jesus anything about the sea, because he knew more than him, anyhow.

"You can see everything. You speak English, so maybe you can see where it is only a mistake or misunderstanding or something."

They chatted for a bit longer. Clint said he'd take responsibility for Sal, but Sal said he didn't mind the jail. He'd stay the night.

Clint said he'd be back in the morning, and went to the hotel to clean up and change. Jorge said the gringo had been in town less than a week, and that he was staying with Armando Cruz. They would be in the bar, for sure!

Clint knew Cruz slightly. He was a big black with the Rasta dredlocks and sometimes had an attitude. Unlike most Rastas, he drank too much and let his mouth run off on him. Most times, he was a normal type of person. He had once had a wife or woman he lived with, but got drunk and beat her up. Her father and four brothers had almost beaten him to death, and she was gone. He went on the wagon for several months and got religion, then drifted back to what he was before

Clint didn't like or dislike him He tended to

avoid him, because he had beat a woman. Drunk or not, Clint could never accept that. He could understand it. He had met a couple of women he thought he'd greatly enjoy smacking in the puss, but that was just an expression, really. He didn't think he could hit a woman.

Well, see what the story was.

Clint found Earl and Armando in the little bar at the end of the main street. They were having a cold beer, maybe the first one. They were both big enough that a few wouldn't affect them to any extent. Armando was careful to stop after four or five. He'd learned his lesson about overdoing it.

Armando Cruz was a twenty five or six year old big black man. Earl Smelters was as big, was about twenty three, and with a complexion and features that showed some black and some white. He was a bit heavy, and reminded Clint of some of the rappers he'd seen on TV. Cruz wore a lot of flashy jewelry, Smelters only a big gold ring and knockoff Rolex.

Clint went to ask if he could join them for a minute to see if he could sort the mess with Sal Santos. Armando waved at a seat, but Earl said there was no mess, so far as he was concerned. The fucking damned Indio had admitted killing his brother. Case closed!

Clint took a dislike to him immediately. He was, apparently, the type who had made up their minds, so don't confuse them with the facts.

"Yo quiere a conoce las factas, no mas," Clint replied.

"Huh?" from Smelters. Armando hid a grin.

"What did I say?" Clint asked.

"Something about no more. No more facts or something."

"So now you can tell everyone I said I don't want more facts, right?"

"Get smart with me and you might get hurt, old man!" Armando grabbed his arm and shook his head. Smelters had started to rise, and sat back down, glaring.

"Nice even temperament, I see. Very reasonable attitude, and always careful about the facts. The type of shithead everyone automatically relates to because he's so amiable and lovable," Clint said innocently. "Armando, if he wants to get in my face before he even knows who I am, let him give it his best shot."

"You ain't nobody, is who you are!" Smelters snarled.

"Shut the fuck up!" Armando demanded. "Clint can kick your stupid ass from here to the bombas and back again and not work up a sweat!

"Clint, he's not usually this way."

"He might not usually *act* this way, but he's always this way," Clint returned. "What? Crack?"

Armando nodded very slightly, and said Clint

knew he didn't believe in using drugs. He didn't say Smelters didn't. Clint sighed, and said, "You going to tell me exactly what Sal said or am I going to go to the station and tell them you're a fucking cokehead and you can't believe a word out of your alligator mouth?"

"Tell them what you want! They have to believe me!"

"Clint is 'they' here," Armando warned. "He's working with the national police. If he tells them you lied, deliberately, under oath, he can have your stupid ass in the pen for three years with a word! You will *not* like the pen here! This isn't Haiti! Just shut the fuck up and answer Clint's questions – and answer them damned straight!"

Smelters looked surprised, then tried to grin, "Okay. I'm an ass. I can't kick the crack. I've tried. God, you don't know how I've tried!

"I'm paranoid about it. I'm defensive about it.

"Believe it or not, I'm a Phd. UCB. The crack's something ... I can't kick it.

"Armando can level me off. I'm not using now, and I'm burning up. I have a hidden death wish because of it. I subconsciously want somebody to blow my head off for me so I'll be free.

"I'll try to answer you.

"I heard about the drowning and someone said the Indio in the store was the brother of the one who drowned. I said something, trying to act like I'm not the ... what I am. Something comforting.

"He said he killed his brother or something. I swear, it sounded like that to me. I was shocked that he'd just admit it. I went to the police and said he admitted it in public, so why was he *in* public, and not locked up?

"That's it. I could have misunderstood, but it's what I really believe. You did that bit with the Spanish to point out I may not have heard what I thought I heard. The guy didn't speak too much English, but ... what he said sounded like he was admitting he killed his brother.

"I knew I should go to the cops and say I may have been wrong, but the paranoia kicked in, and I felt like I was a fool to ever go to the police for anything."

"Try to remember exactly what you said and what he said."

"Well, I said I'd heard about his brother and I was very sorry, and when was the funeral to be, or something. I should have known they wouldn't have planned the funeral that quickly, but I'm ... making excuses. Playing word games with myself, or something. I can't think straight when I'm like this.

"He said he had a grave responsibility for his brother's death, that it was something he had to do. Something like that. I interpreted it as he was saying he had to kill his brother for some reason."

"He said it in English?"

"Yes. I speak very little Spanish. I'm one of the obnoxious type who think everyone who goes to the states should learn English, because it's the language there, then that everyone anywhere *I* go should learn English because I'm spending my money there. I'm also a bigot, as you saw when I made the remark about Indios. I sit here with this nigger, who's my best friend in the world, and make snide remarks about the Indios, who've never done a single damned thing to me."

Armando grinned. "The blacks here are bigots against the Indios a lot. I'm not.

"Who you callin' nigger, honky?"

Clint thought for a few seconds, and shook his head. Armando asked why.

"Because Sal said he was responsible for the interment of his brother. It's something he has to do because it's family."

"What...?" Smelters asked.

"In Spanish, the modifier comes after the word described. It's a 'Man fat' instead of a 'Fat man.'

"Sal said he's responsible for the grave. He has to buy the cemetery plot, or whatever, not that he was responsible for his brother being in that grave. It's something the family does, and he's

Jesus's family.

"He's just learning English and remembered that the modifier comes first in English. He didn't know that 'grave' isn't the modifier, in this case. It's the subject."

Armando nodded. Smelters thought, and said that may well be the case, here. What could he do about it now?

"Just come with me to the station and tell them what really happened. They'll write that investigation showed the statement was misunderstood because of the language barrier, and look elsewhere for the killer."

"What?! Killer?! He *drowned*!" Armando cried.

"Jesus Santos did not drown by accident. It was a calm day, and he was as expert around the water as anyone," Clint replied. "It looks like I do have a job here."

They went to the police station and made a declaration. Sal was released. He went to spend the night with Clint in the hotel. He was willing to sleep in the jail, but Jorge said they needed the space.

In the morning Clint and Sal headed back to Cusapín. They had talked a good while during the night. Jesus didn't have any real enemies that Sal knew of. He had some people he didn't like and who didn't like him, either, but that's life. Even the church Jesus had people who didn't like him.

Clint said that was basically politics. Was his brother concerned with politics?

"He helped some people on the comarca to get votes because he thought they were honest and would help our people. He wanted Indigenos to have more candidates. Not strong, but he did that. He was always disappointed. They were all corrupt after a week in the position they were elected to."

"If our people would put up candidates in the elections they would win in Bocas. We're more than half of the vote."

"We aren't political people, and we don't trust any Indigenos who are. Politicians are politicians, the same as snakes are snakes. They may look different and may hiss different, but they're still snakes."

"Far too true! We have to get candidates who are candidates because the people demand it. We need people who don't want to be part of that. Basilio or Silvio are our chiefs, but they aren't political. They help the people, not themselves."

"They cannot run outside of the comarca. They would know who would be best. It is something to think on."

They went into Cusapín at Clint's dock. Sal went across the town to his home, where his wife and kids greeted him as though nothing had happened. The Indigenos are totally fatalistic about some things. It was an unpleasant part of life that such things happened. Sal still had to arrange for the funeral, which would be there at Cusapín.

Clint spent the day with Tyna and Nito. He would see what he could learn about Jesus in the morning. Sal came to say the funeral would be at twilight the next night in the plot by the sea. When his brother was placed in his final resting place he would speak with Clint about learning *why* he was placed in that final resting place.

<u>*Reason and Reasons*</u>

The funeral was quiet. Several people told of their experiences with Jesus, and all wished him eternal peace.

Clint and Tyana went back to the cabin for the night. He would meet with Sal at dawn to try to find what had happened to Jesus. This wasn't the kind of thing that happened among the Ngobe. If they had a blood fight, it was out in the open, and probably had a damned good reason behind it. They weren't violent people.

It was drizzling rain in the morning, but there wasn't too much wind behind it, so Sal would take the boat out to gather conch for the restaurants in Chiriqui Grande and Bocas Town. He said Jesus was planning to get certain shellfish and such for a big new restaurant in David. The owner had come to him in Chiriqui Grande to try to make a contract, but Jesus told him he couldn't guarantee the amounts because some days the water was bad and he didn't get anything.

"He is from Canada. Mr. Davis. We are to call him Mr. Davis, and he is to call us by our given name."

"What did you say to that crap?" Clint asked, grinning.

"Me? Nothing. He was then dealing with Jesus. Jesus said that was best. It was a business thing, so they would neither use the friendly form. What Mr. Davis didn't know was that he would not get the friendly price, either."

"The difference?"

"Friends, two seventy five. Business, four ten. Friends, fully cleaned. Business, basic clean."

"In other words, he gets it with the inedible part of the foot still attached, so he's paying five something."

Sal nodded.

"I don't think it was an Indio who did this, Sal. Who else was he dealing with that you know of?"

Sal shrugged. "Just the regular people who buy stuff in Chiriqui Grande. I don't know so very much because he always took the things there to sell. I don't care for cities. I was once in David, and it was horrible. All loud noise and bad air and dirty water and ladrones and cars."

"I guess I'll have to go out to Chiriqui Grande. I'm personally certain it was no one from the comarca. There's someone else involved, somehow. I can't picture what a local fisherman would ... know. Maybe he saw or heard something, or maybe he had an argument with someone about something."

"He would tell me if he had a serious argument. He was my brother."

"What have you heard about that Smelters asshole who hangs around with Armando? Earl?"

"I have talked to him a few times for very little. He is a very ignorant man . He is what you call a crackhead. He is here to try to stop using crack, but he is with Armando, who sells crack, so you know exactly where that is going."

"He's educated. A Phd."

"Ignorance is not about what a person knows, ignorance is about what a person does not know."

Clint grinned. That was getting to the point.

"Could Jesus have heard or seen anything about what Smelters is doing that Smelters might think he had to stop?"

"No. Everyone already knows it."

"And Armando? There was never an argument of any kind with Armando?"

"No. Armando is okay. He is not like some. He would be a good person if he would find a better way to survive in life. He does not like what he does, it is because he does not know any other way."

"But he would keep someone like Smelters on crack?"

"Smelters is a psychologist. He knows exactly

what he is doing and what Armando is doing. He is what he appears when he is bad. The false part is when he tries to act like he is a good person with a drug problem. He is trying to find where Armando gets the crack because he wants to take the market from him. His drug problem is not what he wants us to think. Many use crack and are in control of how they act. He is weak and says it is the crack whenever he does something stupid. It is not. It is what he is."

Clint nodded. "Well, I'll be with my wife and baby for awhile, then go to Chiriqui Grande. I'll see what I can find. Whatever it is, it is to remain among them. They are not to involve my people or they will deeply regret it."

He hugged Sal and went back to play with Nito and talk with Tyna. She agreed with him about what he had to do. She understood that, since he was declared a Ngobe, he was a Ngobe, and would accept that he must protect his family, first, his people, second, and himself third.

He loaded a few things on his boat and headed for Chiriqui Grande. He got fuel at the dock there, then went to moor his boat at his accustomed spot on the dock the Indios used. No one would touch anything of his without asking first. It was understood that he still had some gringo ideas, and that "no ownership" didn't apply to quite everything.

Armando was in the little restaurant next to the bar on the main street where the road branched. Clint went in to order coffee and hojaldras.

"Smelters out looking for your wholesaler?"

He laughed. "Yeah. I thought that may be what he was doing. I wasn't sure, but I fixed it so he'd run in circles if he was.

"How did you know?"

"We all know."

"I don't get it, sometimes. Sometimes I think the Indios are friends, then sometimes I think they don't like me."

"They like you. They don't like your business. Keep it away from them, and there's no problem. They think you're a good man trapped in a bad business. Is there any chance whatever that Smelters was behind Jesus's death?"

"No. He was with me the whole day."

"Know anything about this Davis character?"

"The typical condescending idiot who thinks he's richer and smarter than thou, so show him respect, Boy!"

"He was dealing with Jesus for conch?"

"Conch, octopus, langosta. Jesus was working him over because of his attitude. He would have given him a good deal so he'd have a regular income, but the ass can get to you, so he was putting the screws to him, big-time. I think half again to double the price."

"Could he be behind it?"

"*What?!* Cut off my *supply?!*"

Clint laughed, and nodded. "One of those?

"Anyone else you can think of?"

"No. Jesus was a regular guy. I have a hard time thinking it was an accident with him, but I can't think of anyone who had anything against him. Everyone liked him."

"As Sal said, 'Even the church Jesus had people who didn't like him.' There was definitely someone."

Armando shook his head, and grinned. "Sal can come up with the simple obvious fact in such a way as it smacks you up side the head, can't he? That says it all with a minimum of words."

They chatted for a few more minutes, until Smelters came up to complain that it was going to rain again before noon, sure as all hell.

"It's a rain forest area. Of course it's going to rain. What's new?

"Well, Armando, I'll see what I can find in David. (He winked at Armando.) That was Rauz? Hangs around Centro?"

Armando caught on. "No *A*-rauz. Sometimes Centro, sometimes Super ninety-nine, sometimes Rey. Particularly Do-It Center. Sometimes out at

PriceMart. That's the trouble when you're low. He's one place or the other, and you can play hell finding him in a hurry. Just tell him I said I'm feeling regular lately. Just that, okay?"

"I get it. If I come across him I'll give him the message." He nodded at Smelters and walked off. Smelters looked uncertain, then came after Clint.

"What?"

"Uh, did you say you were going to David? Could I catch a ride? I have to go to the Banco General there."

"I'll probably take the bus. I don't like driving in David with today's traffic."

"Oh. Okay. I guess I'll have to do the same."

Clint nodded and went on. He called Tyna and said he was going to David. He didn't think he'd be there long. He went to the bombas and waited for the bus. Smelters came running up, carrying a backpack, and managed to catch the bus as it was driving off. Luckily for Clint, the only seat left was the fold-down by the door. Clint was almost to the rear. He wouldn't have to listen to the ass trying to pump him about what Armando wanted.

As they were approaching Chiriqui, Clint got a phone call. It was Armando. "He got the same bus?"

"Uh-huh. It's almost funny. As big as he is, he

had to take the fold-down by the door. Three hours in that cramped seat that slants to dump you on the floor. Now he'll spend a week looking for someone with one of the most common names here in four or five places across town in every direction from Centro."

"Yeah. If he's in Centro at the same time as one Arauz I know he'll be able to make a deal. He needs an ass-burning like that bunch will give him. I heard a name. Someone who came here with Daniel Davis a time or two. Mick Eggars. They say he's the same type asshole as Davis. It might not mean anything, but I'll let you know anything I hear."

"Thanks, Mando. I have to grab any lead I can."

They soon rang off, and Clint sat back to grin to himself. Smelters had a bad lead and wouldn't know how to find out. He had a lead that may be good or bad, but he'd find out in minutes.

Several people got off the bus at the intersection to meet the Panamá City bus. Smelters was able to move to a seat beside a fat woman with a baby and little girl about two years old. It was a very small improvement for him, but it was an improvement.

Pity.

<u>*Fat Chance!*</u>

Clint checked into the Costa Rica and went across the street to the little Mexican/Honduran restaurante. He had a good meal, then strolled toward Centro. He knew a lot of people and would greet or be greeted every few feet. He reached the corner by Toro Bar where a big fat man from Changuinola was standing. He was a scam artist without much talent and most people avoided him. He spoke excellent English and could become very comfortable using that and his talent for making a good first impression. Instead, he was always working on an angle to screw people out of a few dollars here and there. He had no friends who lasted more than a month or two. He used petty blackmail and stories about how important he had been when Noriega was in power. A lot of people felt sorry for him. Clint didn't. He made his bed with a singleminded purposeness Clint considered pathetic.

Two Indios and a gringo he knew called to him from across the street. He answered. Tonio came from the bar to ask him how he was and about his wife and baby. Big Freddy came by as he was starting to move on toward Wendy Store and they exchanged their joke greeting, calling to anyone close, "Cuidado! Maldito! Maldito!" He asked Clint if he ever caught that crazy woman he was looking for. As Clint passed Gordo, Gordo said, in a sneering voice, "You seem to have a lot of friends here."

"Sure do! And you don't have any anywhere. Think about it!" and walked on. Gordo stood there looking lost.

Asshole!

He went to the corner, bought a tarjeta for his celular, and went toward the park. He greeted a few more people between and in the park. He saw Smelters talking with a local marijuana dealer and grinned to himself. He'd get a lesson two about a gringo crackhead who was that obvious trying to score.

Not much around the park. He saw Lida, a local policewoman and friend, and stopped to chat. She said the cokehead gringo was throwing his name around trying to meet someone. What was that crap about?

"He's trying to find the Arauz who sells crack wholesale. If he's throwing my name around you might accidentally be looking for something in the store across the road when he trips and breaks his nose."

She grinned. "I thought you might appreciate him using your name just about that much.

"Arauz? Fifty of them, all half-penny or less."

"He managed to overhear his local supplier in Chiriqui Grande, who he's trying to shoot out of the saddle, telling me to tell Arauz he's feeling regular. He must have misunderstood the health report."

She laughed. "So he's looking for a wholesaler named Arauz in the Parque Cervantes in David. He'll find ten of them, none the one he wants."

"Uh-huh. And Super ninety-nine. And Rey. And Price-Mart. And others.

She laughed harder. "Maybe I get suspicious after a day or two of that and will run him in for ID certification."

"Know anything about a Daniel Davis and/or Mick Eggars?"

"*Mr*. Davis and *Mr*. Eggars, Girlie! Never heard of them."

"That bad?"

"I'm used to the type. I've never had to use the truncheon, but I think I'd like to have a practice session. Spontaneous!"

"Would they be capable of killing someone over a business deal?"

"I sincerely doubt it. They wouldn't hesitate to hire someone."

"Like who"

"That bunch? Hmmm. Mike Henry or Mick Edwards. Dolega area. Dolega and Las Lomas.

"Thanks, Amiga! I'll check it out!"

He went on into the park and close to Smelters, who looked up and saw him coming. He called, "Hi, Clint!"

Clint walked over and nodded, then said, "Oh, yes! You're that Smellers fellow from Chiriqui Grande! Hi!"

"You didn't send him to find Arauz?" Mano, one of the dealers asked.

"Send him to find who Arauz? There have to be fifty of them in David! For the love of god and country! I'm a *detective*! I don't send anyone to find anyone else! It's what I *do*!"

"Thought so. What's the scam?"

"Got me! Business up to par?"

"Off-season until maybe November. I get by."

"Well, got to do some shopping and try to find someone. New baby, you know!"

"Yeah. Congrats!"

He waved and walked off while Smelters was trying to explain why he said Clint sent him to find anyone. Word would be out in ten minutes and *nobody* was going to deal with Smelters for anything. If he were somehow to accidentally find Armando's source he wasn't going to make any deals.

He was near the terminal and the Dolega bus was going by, so he flagged it and went to the popular bookstore there to ask about locating a Mike Henry who lived in the area. Henry came in once in awhile, but they didn't know where he lived. Maybe toward Anastasia or El Flor.

He had nothing else to do, so walked toward Anastasia, enjoying the countryside. He stopped at the little tienda across from the road to El Flor and asked about Mike Henry. The woman there said he had a small finca on the road to the right behind the bus terminal, such as it was.

He walked on to the road and along it for about two kilometers when he stopped a local peddler and asked about Mike Henry.

"The second road to the left. Right up there."

He walked on and turned into the rocky road. The house was about five hundred meters farther along. There was a small Toyota truck in front.

Clint went to the gate and called, "Buenos!" An attractive black girl came to ask what he wanted.

"Mike around?"

"Yes. His truck's here, so he's here."

"I'd like to speak with him. Business."

A stocky dark man came to ask what the yelling was about. The girl told him the guy at the gate wanted to talk business. He came out. "Yes?"

"I'm Clint Faraday. A good friend of mine died. You were mentioned indirectly."

"Where? When?"

"Chiriqui Grande. Four days ago."

"Not me. Who's the connection who indirectly mentioned me?"

"It was the connection that mentioned you. Not a person."

"Gringo. All business. The type who hire me."

"So it has to be Edwards."

"Probably, but I don't know. He wasn't in the David area four days ago, I think. We only do a thing we're hired to do. It's not personal."

"I blame the one who did the hiring."

"I've heard you don't cut slack. What's going on?"

"If it's some goon who's after some other goon I couldn't care less. Don't leave a mess for someone else to clean up. If it's an innocent bystander there is no slack. Period."

"I can live with that. I've never broken an arm or leg – or offed anyone – who didn't deserve it in spades. The one doing the hiring deserves it from the minute he hires it. Them's the facts of life."

"Um. Good enough for me." He started to walk away, then turned back to call, "Know anything about this Smelters character in the park?"

"Only that I got a call an hour ago that I might be needed. I said not if he's narc or one of those."

"He's not. He's trying to cut other people out of the local supply area."

He nodded and went on to the house. Clint went back and caught the bus.

He decided to wait until morning to go to Las Lomas. It was going to rain for about an hour, so he'd clean up and rest, then go out on the town to talk with people.

He ate a good meal at Boca Chica and went to the regular places he frequented when in David. Three separate girls wanted to spend the night with him. He explained that he was married and a father and that he wouldn't be sleeping around anymore.

He couldn't help comparing these beautiful girls with Tyna. They all fell short, somehow.

He had to be the luckiest guy alive!

He went to the Costa Rica and to bed early. As he went by Toro Bar, Gordo was standing alone on the corner.

Maybe he'd take pity on him and buy him a beer.

Hah! Fat Chance!

Clint ate breakfast at Don Bellos and walked around town for an hour or so until other people were starting to get up.

He learned a lot in the business lately by what he called induction. He'd learned that method from his nextdoor neighbor in Bocas Town, Judi Lum. Mention something in passing in a situation that didn't seem to be a part of what you want and the answer will sometimes tell you a hell of a lot. He'd asked about Smelters. Henry had been contacted. Henry dealt with a certain type. If he'd been contacted that type was worried about what a person who happened to be in Chiriqui Grande and who just happened to report to the police because of a supposed misunderstood remark. It could be because Smelters was involved a lot more than he was led to believe or it could be because he was stupid in the way things worked outside of the US. He damned well didn't know better than to ask about drug dealers in a public park in someone else's name who was known. If he was sent to find a drug dealer he would have a full name and how, when and where to contact him. Certainly no Arauz, dealer or not, would tell him the time of day after that blunder.

Clint remembered Sal's words: "Ignorance is not about what a person knows, ignorance is about what that person does not know," and "Even the church Jesus had people who didn't like him."

Simple, basic, to the point.

He caught the bus for Las Lomas. He got off just over the bridge at the restaurant there. Edwards' type would probably put him more in that kind of place than in the ones in town. He asked the waitress if she knew him when he ordered coffee and hojaldras.

"Mick? Yeah. He comes in at night a lot. He meets with those creepy assholes from the mafia sometimes."

"Local wannabes or the Panamá City type?"

"Local."

Clint shrugged. He wouldn't ask too much or they'd get a report. He asked her if several other people came in who had nothing to do with anything. Gordo came in with two others sometimes and with a big black man. He hung around with the mafia types and they laughed at him behind his back. They made a lot of money by promising him he would get a cut, then using the people he was scamming. They made thousands and he got a pittance.

He soon went on into Las Lomas. Edwards lived just east of the town. He was a zoner, which is a person born in the canal zone. American father, Panamanian mother. Spoke near-perfect English. Would be popular if he didn't think so much of himself. Liked skinny girls with big boobs.

Skinny didn't mean the same here as the states. A woman with a shape like was popular in the states when Clint left would be thought of as skinny. The heavier women were the standard in many places.

Edwards spent a lot of time with the gringos in Volcan and Boquete. The police were interested in him at times, but the neighbors didn't think he was as bad as his reputation. He'd never been in any serious trouble they knew of. He wasn't even the bad-ass type personality.

He wasn't there. He might be in Boquete.

Clint would concentrate on Davis. He could probably work backward to find if he was behind Jesus's murder through other contacts. Edwards wouldn't talk, anyhow. Henry wouldn't if he'd done it.

Daniel Davis, restaurant. He didn't know the name of the restaurant, but knew people in the business. Davis ran several casino/bar/ restaurants and a car wash (?). He lived in a suite in one of the casinos. The Lucky Toss.

Clint found the place and went in to ask for Davis. He was in Panamá City today but was expected back tomorrow afternoon. If it was business George Halley at Double-Ups was in charge.

Clint thought for a minute, then went to find Double-Ups. It was a smaller place that featured a lot of slots and hookers. Halley was a strictly business type in a very expensive cowboy outfit. The boots cost over a thousand dollars. The hat cost more than two hundred. The belt, hat and boots were a matched set. He had a big silver and turquoise tie-clasp on a string tie. Clint didn't doubt that was the only way he ever dressed. It was a lot too much for the place. It was a lot too much for anyplace.

"I'm here because a supplier of seafoods has drowned and his brother wants to know if he should fill the agreement or will you seek another supplier," Clint said.

"Jesus Santos. We know and I've made other arrangements. I was making those arrangements before he died. He had been greatly overcharging me for everything. Anything else?"

"I thought being overcharged for everything was what it was about. That's how laundering works."

He didn't blink. "It's inefficient after the initial establishment of the system. Those who continue it are unwise in business."

The receptionist came in to apologize and ask that Halley sign the check for the vegetables. He signed the check and said to warn Julio about lowering the quality of the produce or he'd find another grower. She took the check and went out.

"These Indios will work you every chance they get! Got to watch them!"

"We treat you the way you treat us. You're just not astute enough to see it."

"We? We who? What are you talking about?!"

"I'm Ngobe. Your superior and know-it-all attitude will be met with lessons to show you don't know a tenth of what you think you do."

He colored and got a very hard set to his mouth. "I think my education guarantees my, as you would call it, astuteness in business."

"In the states, yes. Here, no. It doesn't matter. You're exactly where you want to be, apparently, because you've put yourself there."

"I am, as you say, where I want to be. I have enough to dress well and to enjoy the finer things. You can live on your comarca without a pot or window if that's all you can afford and is where you want to be. I'll stay up here."

"I can probably afford more and better than you.

I don't want it. I don't depend on preying on anyone to get what I want. My son won't be ashamed of how Pops made his.

"I was thinking recently about a man I've met who was standing alone outside of a bar. I once held contempt for him because of what he was, for what he doesn't have. You're in the same trap. I pity him and I pity you.

"I'll get back to my business. Have a nice day."

"Oh? And what do I not have that you have so much of, if I may be so bold?"

"Many of. Friends. I have many friends. You have none. Caio!" He walked out.

So. This character would hire a murder in a picosecond. Just business. If Davis was like him it could even be a business as usual deal for them.

He suddenly stopped and turned to stare at the entrance. That could be behind it! He had to find who delivered the seafoods to the casinos!

<u>*So What?*</u>

Clint got back to Chiriqui Grande a little after dark. He called Tyna and chatted awhile, then booked a room at the hotel. He had to find the person who delivered the seafoods from Jesus to those casinos. That money they were laundering came from somewhere, plus that ass, Halley, was out to make a buck any way he could. That just might include side deals.

In the morning he went to the bombas for a very early breakfast. Armando was there, so he joined him at the table.

"Waiting for Smelters to come back?" he asked.

"Yeah. He said he finished his banking stuff and was coming back. I suppose he's out of medicine and can't score any in David for some reason."

"Maybe because he was telling the locals he was looking for Somebody Arauz for me. I asked them why the hell a detective would send some schmuck to look for someone. It's what I *do*!"

"So now the shithead can't hope to find my supplier and no one will deal with him. Maybe it's time I actually do get him off the stuff, huh?"

"Yeah. No reason you should deal with him

either.

"You get the stuff from Davis or, my candidate, Halley?"

He laughed. "That jackass idiot couldn't find the source in a year, you find it in a couple of hours. Only Halley. Davis doesn't know anything about it."

"I'm, as I told the parque bunch, a detective. It's what I *do*!

"Who was delivering the conch to the casino?"

"Berto Jimenez."

They chatted. Armando was waiting when the early bus from David came in. Smelters got off and came over to the table to say he finished his banking deal in David.

"I have to go to Changuinola for today and most of tomorrow. Business," Armando told him with a wink at Clint.

"Er, could I talk to you a minute in private?"

"You can say whatever you want to in front of Clint. What?"

"I, uh, I'm sort of low in medicine. Can I score a little until you're back?"

"No got today! That's why I've got to go the hell to Changuinola."

"Oh. Maybe I'll go with you."

"Now look, Earl. You went to David and threw Clint's name around. Every dealer in the country gets paranoid about that kind of thing. It could have been almost anyone but Faraday. If you show up in Changuinola while I'm there I won't be able to conduct any business.

"Why would you do anything that stupid?"

"I heard you tell Clint to give Arauz a message. I'm out of stuff! I was trying to score!"

"The ones you were telling Clint sent you could have gotten it. Now none of them will ever deal with you again. I might even get orders not to deal with you or my source dries up.

"You have a source in Costa Rica. Maybe you should just go there. Nobody in Panamá will ever deal with you again.

"Christ almighty damn! Anybody in the world but Clint Faraday and it would be, 'So what?' With him, it's time to close the store."

"But Faraday's their friend! They said so!"

"They don't know why he's in David. You're throwing his name around. He's acting like he doesn't know you because he doesn't want them to know why he's there.

"Think about it! You get paranoid all the time and all they could tag you for is using, and they don't much give a hot shit here. What would you do?"

"I'd get paranoid. Shit! I don't know what to do! Would they really cut you off if you sell to me?"

"In a heartbeat! They don't take chances."

"Oh, shit! Maybe I'll go back to San José, but it's getting scary there is why I came here. Shit!"

"Maybe that would be best. For both of us.

"I'll be back tomorrow afternoon, I hope. We can talk then. The bus is about ready to leave." He went to the bus and got on.

"Clint ... I'm sorry! You can't score just a little for me, can you?"

"I never get involved is why they trust me. I'll have to tell them that I wasn't in David looking for you, that you weren't involved in why I was there that I know of. They'll still never trust you again."

He looked like he would cry. He turned around and flagged the taxi out front and went to get in. Clint got in and said to take him to the hotel.

Smelters didn't say anything else on the ride to downtown. He got out in the front of Armando's rooming house and told the cab to come back there for him after he delivered Clint. He would pay him to take him to Sixola border crossing. He had to get to Costa Rica fast.

Clint went a few blocks toward the docks and got out. Beto's little truck was outside the aduana gates.

Clint went to the aduana shack, but Beto just parked there most nights because no one was going to mess with the truck right against the fence. There was a guard three meters away! Beto was in the rooming house down the block to the right.

Clint went to sit in the restaurant across the street for coffee. He called Tyna and talked for about twenty five minutes. Beto came out and he called to him. He came in to share the table.

"You delivered the conch and other stuff to the casinos in David?"

"Just the Double-Up. They took them to all the other places from there."

"You saw or heard something the last time you were there or the time before."

"Not that I recall. It was normal. Drop the stuff and get the check."

"The same people as always were around when you delivered?"

"Yeah."

"You pick up the stuff for Armando there?"

He suddenly looked a little scared. "Armando?"

"He told me about it. To me, that's a big 'So what?' is all. Beto, something happened or you saw or heard something that Jesus died for. The check was made out to him?"

"Yes. Always."

"The woman brought it to you?"

"Yes. She was there with that man from another

club and didn't know how much it would be until I unloaded all the stuff. She made the check on the machine in the office and went in back to get it signed."

"The man from another club?"

"He was there two or three times before. She called him Big Carlos. I think he runs another business and is a boss or something because he told her what to do. He didn't ask."

"What's this Big Carlos look like?"

"He's Colombian. Big and has a lot of jewelry, but not real flashy. It's expensive and you know it. He has a tattoo of a tiger on his arm when his coat isn't on. It doesn't seem like the kind of thing a man who wears such expensive clothes would have, but he probably got it before he made the money or something."

"Big Carlos. A Colombian. It may be important that he was there. Did he do or say anything unusual?"

"No, not really. I got the check. I was expecting a little package for Armando, but it wasn't there. Sra. Votrez, the woman there, said there was nothing to take back. That was all."

"Thanks. I think I see what happened.

"Beto, don't let on that you saw or heard anything or that you even went there for Jesus or Armando. It could be dangerous."

Beto nodded. Clint called Tyna to say he had to go back to David. Stay on the comarca until he returned. He was getting worried about the type of people he was after and they might kidnap her if she was in Chiriqui Grande or something. He got his car and headed for David.

<u>*Don't Say the Wrong Thing*</u>

Clint got into David at four in the afternoon and checked into the Palacio Imperial. The place was a lot better now that it was cleaned up and newly painted. It had always been comfortable enough, though on the lower end. It was inexpensive and located a bit out of downtown, not far from Mae Lewis Hospital. It also wasn't too very far from Double-Ups.

He had to make some kind of arrangements with his friends in the police. He didn't want any innocent people caught up in the mess he felt he was going to be uncovering. He wanted only the people responsible tagged and out of the picture. He wanted to get the one responsible for Jesus's murder caught in an eye-for-an-eye way. That the rest of them would be caught for lesser things was only a side-effect. They were caught up in it because they were in it. They took the implied risks with their eyes wide open and their mouths, supposedly, tightly shut. That way they wouldn't say the wrong thing at the wrong time and in the wrong place. They would not say a thing that was misunderstood that could lead to what this had become.

"Ignorance is not because of what a person knows, ignorance is because of what a person does not know."

This was a statement that was made silently. Clint remembered the old saw, "What you do makes a louder statement than what you say." In one of Dave's science fiction books he had put it as, "Thy statement may be disposed of with a word and wave of the hand while thy silence is forever writ in stone!" or something such.

Weird. He was philosophical?

He had to try to find Big Carlos, the Colombian. He suspected the part he ran wasn't in Panamá to any extent. It was on the basic supply end. Halley had been operating on supply-side economics, and had gotten much too directly involved in the process. He was a typical accountant-type who had found a process. He watched those TV shows about Las Vegas and dressed like the people in those things. He tried to act like those people, then lost sight of the way they operated.

They did not get involved in anything that could tag them. That's what underlings are for. Always have a goat handy. That meant ... something was missing here. Jesus was dead because Halley or Big Carlos thought he knew something he didn't know. He wasn't even the right victim.

It probably wouldn't have led to anything if a Ngobe hadn't died and if Clint Faraday didn't decide, long ago, that his people would not go unavenged for such things. That applied to any innocent person, not only Ngobe. The fact that Jesus was a Ngobe made it more definite and more urgent, is all.

Clint went to the bar-restaurant, Coco on the Green, two blocks from the hotel, for a good meal and to talk. Several of the people there went to the Double-Ups at times. They knew Halley and laughed at him behind his back. He was just a lot of flash and ostentation. He wanted everybody there to know he was the boss. Davis was there sometimes. He was as bad with attitude, though he didn't go for the ostentation. Only one had ever seen Big Carlos, who was never around the place at night. He was only in David a couple of days per month. They had heard of him, some saying he was supposedly running the place for a big syndicate from the USA. The zonies had built the places and were actually in charge because the law said they had to be owned and operated by Panamanians. They were zonies. They were born in Panamá and were Panamanian citizens.

Clint went back to the hotel after a couple of hours and sacked out. He had it pieced together in a way that took everything he'd learned into consideration. He wasn't going to be able to tag Jesus's murderer directly, but he had a way to handle it indirectly. It would also clear up a sore on the face of the country.

In the morning Clint went to the police station to talk with Tonio about what he'd learned. He wanted a deal where people like Armando and Beto wouldn't get into trouble. Tonio agreed that something that would stop the trade in a big way made that a no-brainer. He'd see they weren't mentioned in any way.

"Tonio, we have to find a non-Indio who gets the stuff there. The Indios don't understand what the big deal is and are not doing anything they feel is illegal or wrong. They are picking up a package and delivering it. You won't find one of them who are dealing in any way.

"How do we work it?"

"The casinos are watched. When a known or suspected criminal goes there, it's noted. We did arrest one who went there regularly from near Santiago. He delivered beef. He was stopped at a checkpoint on his way back to Santiago and had two kilos of cocaine under the seat of his truck. He never broke and told us where he got it.

"I think he was dealing. He picked up his own stuff. He, of course, is off the route for the next six years. There isn't any shortage of cocaine in

Santiago, so someone else has the pickup. All we have to do is find who and when there's to be a pickup. We'll leave it to you to arrange for us to intercept in the right place and at the right time. It may be a month or it may be tomorrow.

"I'll check other regular deliveries and the drug action in the places they come and go from."

"I'll try to find someone, too. I want this done!"

They chatted awhile. Clint went outside and called Armando and said he hoped he had a good supply because this end was going to be shut down – and did he know anyone else who used that operation?

"Killer Dan, Bocas. You know him. Around the Barco Hundido and the Mondo Tatu all the time. Big black man with dredlocks. He goes there on the fifteenth of the month. Supposed to be selling them crab meat, but there aren't enough crabs around Bocas for one dinner, much less for a restaurant.

"Today's the fourteenth. You lucked out. He's a shithead violence freak so long as he has three buddies with him, so be careful."

"Thanks, Mando. Sorry to cut your supply, but they shouldn't have involved an innocent person, much less a Ngobe."

"I know. It's okay. The season won't start for three months and I have enough put away to tide me through."

They soon rang off and Clint went back inside to Tonio's office to say, "Tomorrow. Killer Dan from Bocas. Big black bodybuilder type."

Tonio took out a thick file and leafed through it until he drew out a sheet.

"Clarence Axel Daniels, twenty eight, Bocas del Toro, Bocas del Toro, 2012 Mitsubishi truck, sells crab meat ... from Bocas? Really? ... every fifteenth of the month. Usually has Fonzi Veras or Elvis Quiroz along. Suspected street dealer in marijuana. Parents from Jamaica and talks more Jamaican than US English. Usually talks Wadi-Wadi."

"Yeah. Him."

"So! How is it to go down?"

"He's going to have an accident as he drives out. Find an old junker."

"Will do! There's going to be a cop right across the street who's just happening to be passing! His luck will suck tomorrow!

"I'll have him noted crossing the checkpoint in Hornitos. We can have it set up and ready."

"I think I'm going to be coming back to David from Dolega just about then and will be passing when ... no. I'm going to be talking with a Mr. Daniel Davis at the Lucky Toss when the news comes in. I can decide right then how deep he is in it."

They got together with a special squad to make their plans. These were six men Tonio knew and could trust. Word about it was *not* getting out before it went down!

Clint finally went to the Palacio Imperial and to change and go into David to spend some time chatting with people he knew. He called Tyna to chat for awhile. He was getting too domesticated. He wanted to be home with his wife and kid.

He sacked out a little early. Tomorrow just might be a very interesting day!

<u>*Surprise!*</u>

Clint waited until almost three when the call came in that Killer Dan and Elvis Quiroz just came through the checkpoint. They'd be in David in a little less than an hour.

Clint dressed up a little and headed for the Lucky Toss. He went in forty five minutes after the call from the checkpoint. Killer Dan drove fast enough that he was just coming across the bridge at Las Lomas.

Clint sat around for ten minutes or so, then was shown into a fancy wood-paneled office. Davis was sitting behind a huge polished cherry wood desk

"What can I do for you, Mr. Faraday?"

"I'm investigating the murder of Jesus Santos in Chiriqui Grande. I'm told that you met with him several times and had arranged for seafood shipments from him?"

"*Murder*?! Er, yes. I spoke with Jesus a few times.

"Murder?"

"Yes. He was an expert seasoned fisherman who knew the waters and ways of the area. There was no storm nor high wind. It was a calm day. No one who knew him could accept that he had any accident out there.

"No one who knew him believes anyone in the area had any reason to fight with him, much less to kill him.

"That leaves people not from the area. You are one of those people, so I have to ask you if you ever noted anything at all about what could be behind it. Did he ever mention anyone here in David? From any other place?"

"You can't seriously think I'm a suspect!"

"I only think he may have said something to you about someone from David."

"No, well, except somebody named Beto who came here to David at times or something, but I thought he was speaking about a person there at Chiriqui Grande."

"Yes. I've spoken with Beto. He knows of no one who...."

"Mr. Davis! The telephone! There is trouble at Double-Ups! A lot of police officers!" a secretary screeched, running into the room. Davis grabbed the phone and yelled, "What the hell...? George?"

"Oh. Votrez. They are doing what?"

"Why?"

"Where are you? Can they hear you?"

"What drug sale? I know nothing...."

"Is he crazy?! What the hell?! How much?"

"Only that much, you can claim he must have picked it up from someone in the casino. I want to know why anyone had any of it."

"They won't find you there. You may have to stay awhile. Do you have food and water?"

"I'll see what I can do. Call later." He hung up.

"Some kind of problem at another of my places. An employee or friend of one or something had some, uh, counterfeit money and the police raided the place looking for it or something.

"I really must see what I can do about this. You will understand."

Clint stood and nodded. He went out and called Tonio as soon as he was sure he couldn't be seen or overheard.

"Tonio! Do you have Votrez? The woman in Halley's office?"

"No. She isn't here. We can't find any drugs, either."

"She's there. She called Davis. She's somewhere you won't find and probably has to stay there for a day or two. Does she have food and water?"

"I see. How will we find it?"

"I'll be there right away. You have everything else you need? Halley? Killer Dan?"

"Yes. Killer Dan is spilling his guts to try to

stay out of jail. He doesn't think he'll live an hour if he's put in there because he knows too much about too many people."

He talked while he drove to Double-Ups. Killer Dan and Elvis were sitting on the floor inside the door in steel shackles. Clint asked, "Votrez. The woman. Where was she when you were here?"

"Right there at the office. She got the stuff and brought it to me."

"From the office? She didn't leave?"

"No."

"Then she's somewhere you get to from here." He went into the office to look around. Halley was seated behind his desk in handcuffs.

"You going to tell us where she is or do we spend a few days starving her out?" He only got a glare in answer.

Clint went around the room testing the shelves and so forth for a hidden entrance to something, but there wasn't anything. He went back into the reception room and looked around. There was a large walk-in safe and a door that led into a small bathroom. He checked the bathroom, but there wasn't anything there.

He tried the safe door. It was locked.

It was also the only place she could be. He told Tonio that was the only possible place, so far as he could see. Tonio told Halley to open the safe.

He refused. Clint said to turn off the electric in the safe. The wires were right there. It would also turn off the ventilator.

Halley said there was nothing in the safe but the last two days' receipts. He opened it.

There was nothing in it. Clint walked around and shook his head. He checked over the entire thing and found an alarm set panel. The alarm was set inside the safe?

The door was closed. Halley opened it and the alarm didn't go off. The control box was inside. Halley hadn't even looked at it.

"You gonna tell us the combination or do we get a crew in here and cut our way in?" Tonio asked him. "If cutting in turns off the air, you'll be charged with her murder."

He looked around, then went to punch a number series. There was a "Click!" and a panel above slid open. Clint started to reach for the opening and there was a shot from behind him followed, by an immediate shot that rang off the wall six inches beside his head. A Glock 70 dropped from the hole, then Votrez slid out and dropped at his feet. Tonio was standing behind him with his service pistol pointed at the hole. He was where he could see inside. Clint was too directly below.

"She was almost fast enough. I got her as she shot. You would be the one laying there if I'd missed!”

“Cripes!” was all that Clint could think of to say.

“She’s alive. I didn’t hit her in a fatal spot. I guess I should have, but I want the lady to answer a few questions.”

“You and me both,” Clint answered. He swung up to the opening and looked inside. “There has to be a ton of the stuff in here! There’re millions in cash, too. How big *was* this thing?”

“Mr. Halley will answer all your questions very quickly and truthfully or he will be put in the prison here to be held for trial. He was selling drugs out the back door. I really *really* don’t think that will be looked on kindly,” Tonio said. “Get cameras in here, count that money and list it and remove it, then weight every milligram of the drug and be sure it’s accounted for. There had better not be anything at all missing when we recount and weigh at the station.

“Get the woman some medical attention. We’ll take Mr. Halley in and question him, then speak with Snra. Votrez for confirmation.

“Mr. Halley. Is Big Carlos the head hombre in Colombia only or here too?”

“What are you talking about? *She’s* the head of the whole operation, both here and in Colombia! Carlos is her boyfriend.”

"And she let you sell little packages out the back door?" Clint asked.

"I didn't sell anything out the back door! *She* did!" he squealed. "My god! I wouldn't have lived ten minutes!"

"She has millions stashed up there and she sold a thousand here and a thousand there? Get real!" Clint snarled.

"My god! I swear! I never sold one ounce of anything!"

"Greedy bitch, eh what?" Tonio asked.

"Rawther, Oi'd saigh!" Clint answered. "Shall we clean this mess up? I want to go home.

"Oh, shit! Who had Jesus knocked off?"

"Carlos. He feared Jesus had made him for the drugs when Votrez wouldn't deliver them with him there," Halley answered. "I told him it would come back to slap him in the face. The Indio wouldn't ever say anything. It wouldn't register with them."

"He made another mistake there," Clint said. "It wasn't Jesus who delivered the stuff. It was ... another Indio. It registered, he just didn't give a hot damn.

"Where will I find Big Carlos?"

"Probably at Votrez's place. She has the penthouse at Skylark."

"I'll come to the station after I make a call. You

don't suppose she called him, do you?"

"There's a good chance she didn't," Halley said. "He'd come here and give her away by being here. He's not the brightest star in the galaxy."

"I'll have him picked up," Tonio promised. "You come with us to the station. I think you have this figured better than we do."

Clint sighed and said he'd come. Not much else to do, and he did want to get back home.

They went to the station where they got a lot of information about the operation. This end was closed, but there wasn't anything they could do about the Colombian end.

Tonio got a call about twenty minutes later. The two officers sent to pick up Big Carlos were in the hall. Carlos was inside and had an automatic weapon of some sort and was shooting up the place. The door was splinters and they'd barely managed to dive out of the way. They were now pinned down in the hall.

"You have Big Carlos's number?" Clint asked Halley, who was sitting staring in horror at the phone.

"Six six four seven six five oh oh three."

Clint called. After four rings Carlos answered.

"Hey, shithead!" Clint greeted. "You're in a penthouse with no way out except the elevator and stairs that you can't hope to survive trying for. Stop being an idiot. Put the Uzi down and come on out. If I have to come up there you're going to be begging me to let you die."

There was no answer. Carlos had rung off.

"I'll be damned!" Tonio said half a minute later. "He just threw an AK-forty seven out the door and is standing there with his hands on his head!"

"He watches too many TV movies," Clint said. "Let's finish this so I can get home."

"Okay."

They worked awhile, then went to the hospital room where Votrez was swearing about everything. She had been cheated out of what was rightfully hers! She'd have every cop in David hit! They didn't know who they were fooling with! She could buy and sell the whole damned city for pocket change! She had a team of lawyers that would make fools out of them all and she would end up with everything any of them had!

Clint walked out and went back to the Palacio Imperial, got his things together, and headed back to Chiriqui Grande and his wife and kid.

Clint laid back in the big hammock and gazed dreamily across the Caribbean. He and Tyna were taking his son to Tula next, then would probably stay in Bocas Town for a few days or weeks, then would return to the paradise that was Cusapín.

Tyna came out to tease at him. They played and petted awhile, then she went back inside.

His celular buzzed. It was Tonio.

"Clint? Tonio here. Just thought you might like to know what happened with our little group of businessmen.

"Halley spilled his guts and got a sort of witness protection. It won't work and he'll end up dead within a couple of months. Ditto Davis, though he didn't have too much important to say. Big Carlos got fifteen years."

"Votrez?"

"I think she's totally nuts! She has a panel of no less than twelve lawyers who are finding the most ridiculous things to cause more continuances and delays that you ever heard of. She's managed to buy some pretty comfortable mattresses and a big plasma TV for her cell. She has people bringing her fancy food from the best restaurants. She tried to bribe Judge Henriquez with a million dollars or so to let her get out on bail long enough for her to get to Colombia. I told him he ought to take it. We could see she had an accident crossing the border.

"Armando Cruz was offered a job as interpreter for the government offices in Bocas Province. He does speak excellent English and there are more and more gringos there. He makes as much as he did with the drugs and doesn't have to put up with crackheads quite all the time.

"I'm being transferred to Panamá City, so I don't suppose we'll be working together much. I do want to stay in touch, though.

"That's about it."

"I'll be sorry to see you go. Things are perfect here. My kid's the smartest and handsomest on the comarca and my wife's the dream woman other women wish they could be. I'm the only sour note, so I stay in the background.

"We're going to Tula for a few weeks, then to Bocas Town, then back here to paradise.

"I guess nothing exciting will happen for awhile now. I can use the rest!"

"You're as nuts as Votrez! Tell Tyna and Nito I said hello and that I'm thinking of them and envying you.

"Oh, yeah! We got a call from Costa Rica. Some Professor Smelters wants to have us thank you for getting him off of crack. He said that by the time he got there he was down enough to be able to think and hasn't been on it again.

"Don't know what that's about."

"You don't want to."

C. D. Moulton's works are available on most major outlets as printed or e-books. CD writes the CD Grimes, PI mysteries, the Det. Lt. Nick Storie mysteries, the Clint Faraday mysteries, the Flight of the Maita science fiction series, books on orchid culture and many others of many types. Mystery, adventure, intrigue, science fiction, fantasy, paraormal, mild erotica, and factual.